X GAMES

Moto X Best Trick

by Connie Colwell Miller

Reading Consultant:
Barbara J. Fox
Reading Specialist
North Carolina State University

Content Consultant:
Ben Hobson
Content Coordinator
Extreme Sports Channel
United Kingdom

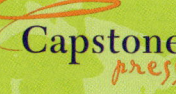

Mankato, Minnesota

Blazers is published by Capstone Press,
151 Good Counsel Drive, P.O. Box 669, Mankato, Minnesota 56002.
www.capstonepress.com

Copyright © 2008 by Capstone Press, a Capstone Publishers company. All rights reserved. No part of this publication may be reproduced in whole or in part, or stored in a retrieval system, or transmitted in any form or by any means, electronic, mechanical, photocopying, recording, or otherwise, without written permission of the publisher. For information regarding permission, write to Capstone Press, 151 Good Counsel Drive, P.O. Box 669, Dept. R, Mankato, Minnesota 56002. Printed in the United States of America

Library of Congress Cataloging-in-Publication Data
Miller, Connie Colwell, 1976–
  Moto X Best Trick / by Connie Colwell Miller.
  p. cm. — (Blazers. X Games)
  Summary: "Describes the X Games Motocross Best Trick event, including how the event is performed, judging, tricks, and star riders" — Provided by publisher.
  Includes bibliographical references and index.
  ISBN-13: 978-1-4296-1290-6 (hardcover)
  ISBN-10: 1-4296-1290-8 (hardcover)
  1. Stunt cycling — Juvenile literature. 2. Motocross — Juvenile literature. 3. ESPN X Games — Juvenile literature. I. Title. II. Series.
GV1060.154 M55 2008
796.6 — dc22   2007032848

Essential content terms are bold and are defined at the bottom of the page where they first appear.

Editorial Credits
Carrie A. Braulick and Abby Czeskleba, editors; Bobbi J. Wyss, set designer;
  Alison Thiele, book designer; Jo Miller, photo researcher

Photo Credits
AP Images/Jack Dempsey, cover; Jae C. Hong, 26; Bill Ross, 15;
  Mark J. Terrill, 6, 14, 25
Corbis/Bo Bridges, 28–29; Icon SMI/Tony Donaldson, 21;
  Reuters/Phil McCarten, 8 ZUMA/Andrew Heritage, 12–13
Getty Images Inc./Doug Pensinger, 17;
  WireImage/Phillip Ellsworth, 5, 7, 9, 22–23
SportsChrome, Inc./Mike Ehrmann, 11, 18

The publisher does not endorse products whose logos may appear on objects in images in this book.

1 2 3 4 5 6 13 12 11 10 09 08

Table of Contents

A Ride to Remember 4

Best Trick Basics 10

Going for the Gold 16

Best Trick Legends 24

Best Trick Course Diagram 22

Glossary 30

Read More 31

Internet Sites 31

Index 32

A Ride to Remember

On August 4, 2006, Travis Pastrana sped off a **jump** on the Motocross Best Trick course. X Games fans fixed their eyes on the talented rider. They expected a truly amazing trick.

jump (JUHMP) — a ramp that riders use to perform tricks

Travis Pastrana

Pastrana flew into a backflip. Fans had seen that trick many times. But Pastrana's next move shocked them. He did another complete backflip and landed perfectly!

No Best Trick competitor had ever done a double backflip. The crowd went wild. The amazing trick earned Pastrana the gold medal.

Best Trick Basics

Like other **freestyle motocross** riders, Best Trick riders do tricks in midair. There is one big difference between Best Trick and freestyle motocross riders. Best Trick riders are judged on only one wild trick.

freestyle motocross (FREE-stile MOH-toh-kross)—a motocross style that includes tricks and jumps

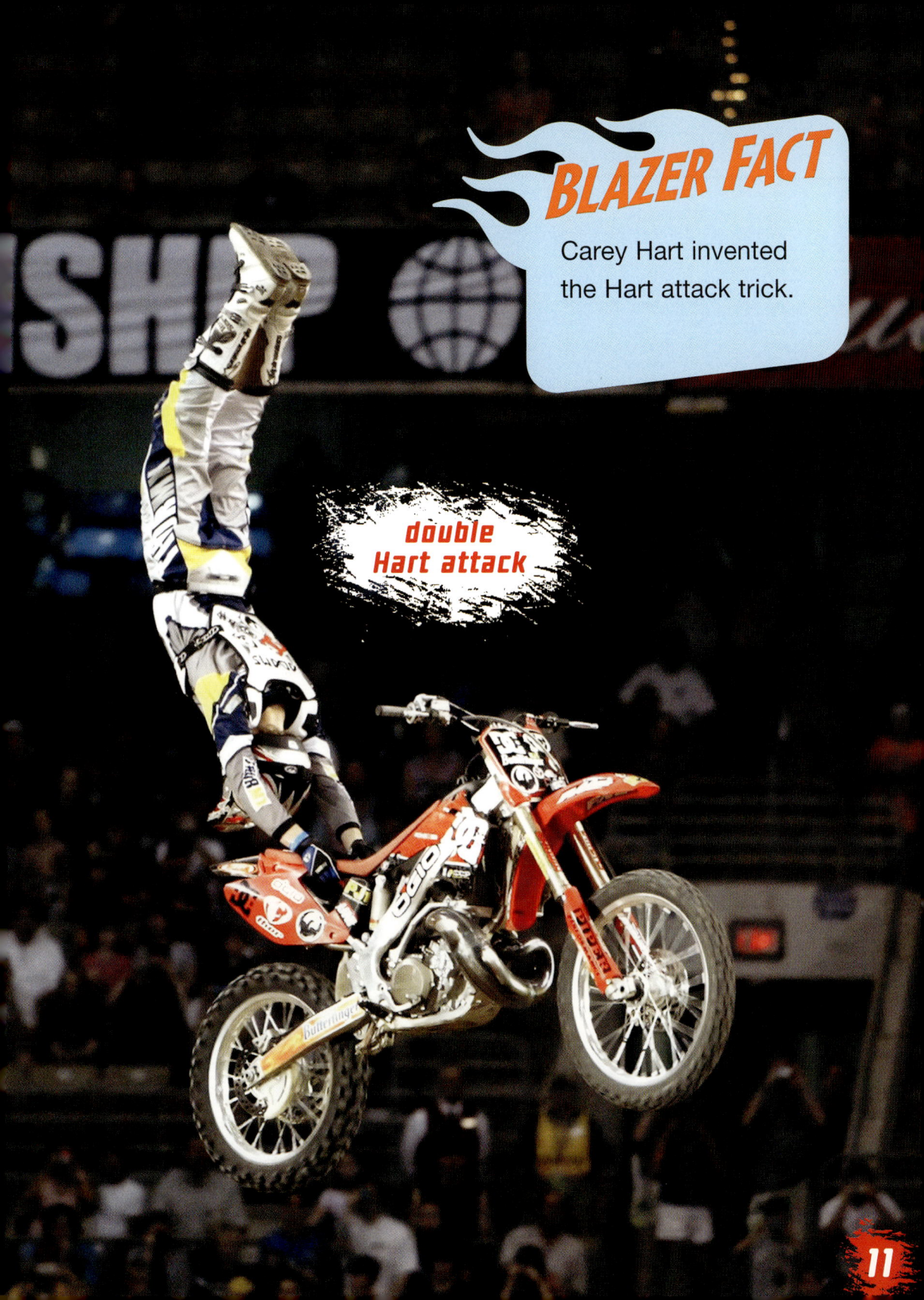

BLAZER FACT
Carey Hart invented the Hart attack trick.

double Hart attack

BLAZER FACT

At the Winter X Games, Best Trick jumps are made of snow.

Best Trick riders choose one of three jumps for their trick. The largest jump has a 90-foot (27-meter) gap!

rock solid

Once Best Trick riders catch big air, the real action begins. Tricks like the **rock solid** get lots of attention. Riders often combine tricks for one really awesome move.

rock solid (ROK SOL-id) — a trick where the rider completely lets go of the bike in midair

BLAZER FACT

Motocross Best Trick is sometimes called Motocross Big Air.

Going for the Gold

Best Trick riders take two turns, or **runs**, on the course. Each run gives riders a chance to show their very best trick.

run (RUHN) — a rider's turn on the course

heel clicker

Judges give the riders a score from zero to 100. The judges rate the riders on creativity, riding style, and trick difficulty.

The highest score from the two runs determines where a rider places. All riders want the gold medal. The top three riders win large cash prizes.

Best Trick Course Diagram

landing area

Best Trick Legends

Best Trick athletes battle it out every year at the X Games. Top Best Trick riders include Mat Rebeaud, Blake Williams, and Nate Adams.

Jeremy Stenberg

In 2005, Jeremy Stenberg beat Pastrana for the gold medal. Stenberg performed a 90-foot (27-meter) backflip. This was the longest backflip ever!

Best Trick is a sport that changes every year. Stars invent new tricks all the time. These legends keep fans wondering what bold move will be next.

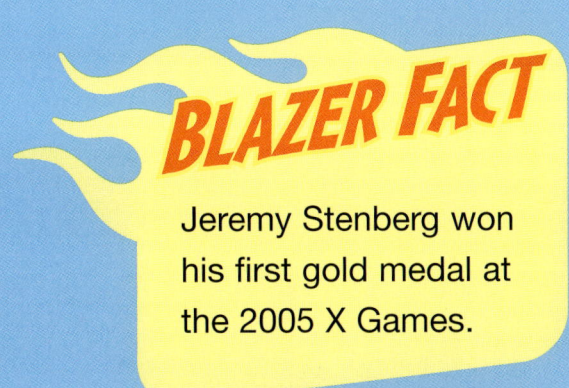

BLAZER FACT

Jeremy Stenberg won his first gold medal at the 2005 X Games.

Glossary

course (KORSS) — an area where a sport is played; motocross best trick riders have a three-jump course.

creativity (kree-ay-TI-vuh-tee) — the ability to think of new ideas

freestyle motocross (FREE-stile MOH-toh-kross) — a motocross style that includes tricks and jumps

invent (in-VENT) — to think up or create something new

jump (JUHMP) — a ramp that riders use to perform tricks

rock solid (ROK SOL-id) — a freestyle motocross trick where the rider completely lets go of the bike in midair

run (RUHN) — a rider's turn on the course

Read More

Levy, Janey. *Motocross Tricks.* Motocross. New York: PowerKids Press, 2007.

Schaefer, A. R. *Extreme Freestyle Motocross Moves.* Behind the Moves. Mankato, Minn.: Capstone Press, 2003.

Sievert, Terri. *Travis Pastrana: Motocross Legend.* Dirt Bikes. Mankato, Minn.: Capstone Press, 2006.

Internet Sites

FactHound offers a safe, fun way to find Internet sites related to this book. All of the sites on FactHound have been researched by our staff.

Here's how:
1. Visit *www.facthound.com*
2. Choose your grade level.
3. Type in this book ID **1429612908** for age-appropriate sites. You may also browse subjects by clicking on letters, or by clicking on pictures or words.
4. Click on the **Fetch It** button.

FactHound will fetch the best sites for you!

Index

Adams, Nate, 24

courses, 4, 16

fans, 4, 7, 27
freestyle motocross, 10

gaps, 13
gold medal, 9, 20, 26, 27

Hart, Carey, 11

judges, 19
jumps, 4, 12, 13

Pastrana, Travis, 4, 7, 9, 26

Rebeaud, Mat, 24
runs, 16, 20

scoring, 19, 20
Stenberg, Jeremy, 26, 27

tricks, 4, 7, 9, 10, 11, 13, 14, 16, 19, 27
   double backflip, 7, 9
   Hart attack, 11
   rock solid, 14

Williams, Blake, 24